The Flying Orchestra

Written and illustrated by

Clare McFadden

UQP

Some days are so windy
that even the angels
lose their balance from
the top of City Hall.

It's always a day like this
when the Flying Orchestra
blows into town.

Their concert program
is a busy one –

a violin solo
when someone misses their train,

a symphony at the airport

for a traveller coming home,

a concerto

when someone stays awake
all night thinking,

and a sonata

for a sad moment
at a birthday party.

The Flying Orchestra always plays

when a baby is born.

And every single
day they play
at dusk

and at dawn

(even when the percussionist
has a head cold).

They go on outings to the seaside

and play at lunchtime
when the ocean sparkles
and glitters in the sun.

They fly out to the country

and play under a sky
milky with stars.

The Flying Orchestra will play

when someone learns to
ride a bike,

cooks dinner for six,

or has lost their way
in the middle of
a cold and dark night.

SALE
25

And wherever they are,
the Flying Orchestra play their
best and most beautiful music

for no reason in particular,
but just because someone is listening.

Some days are so windy that even the angels lose their balance from the top of City Hall.

It's always a day like this
when the Flying Orchestra
blows out of town.

They fly far, far away –

over cities, towns and seas.
It's quiet for a while. And then ...

the music starts again,

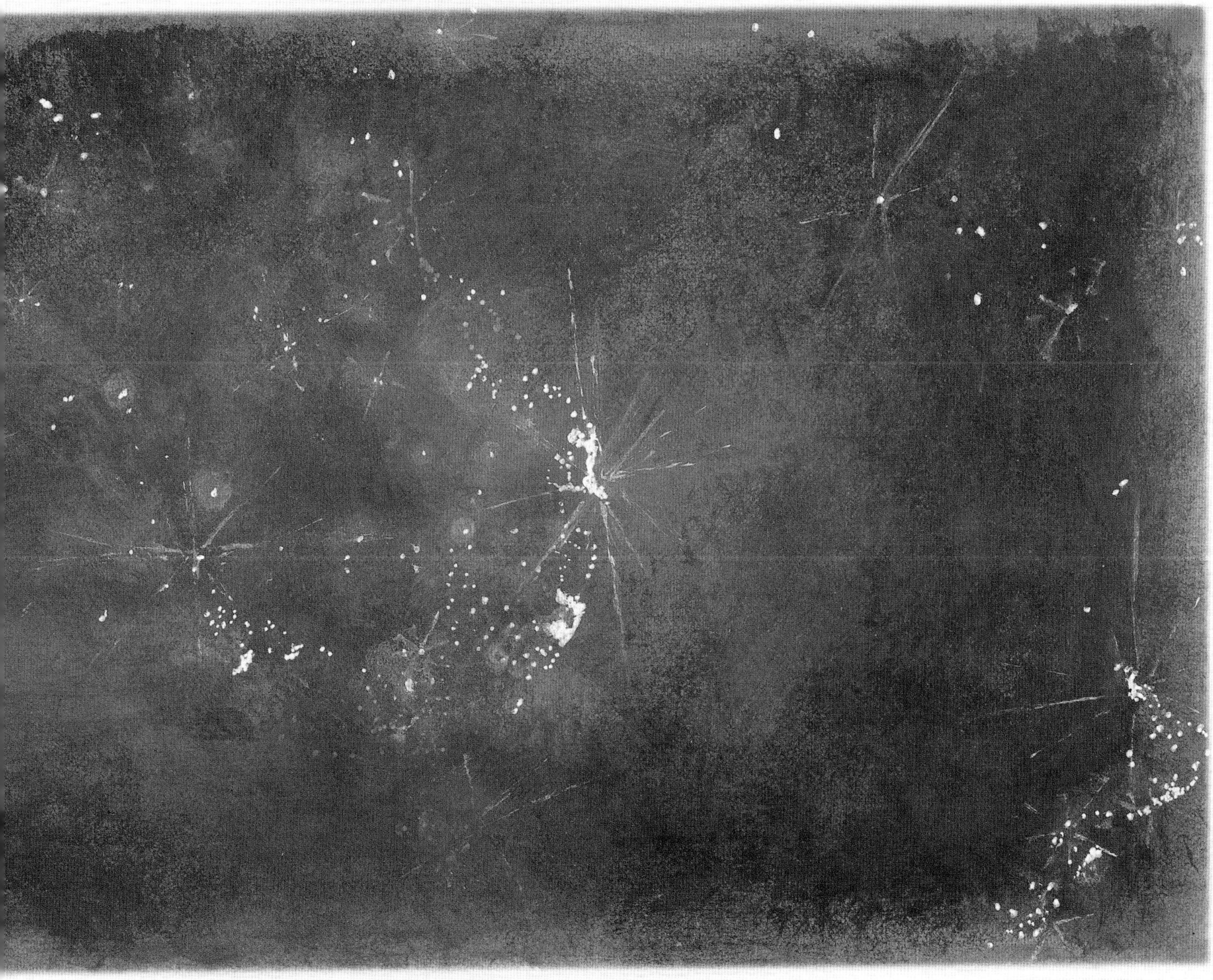

as beautiful as before,
in all the places they have been.

Music to listen to ...

... when someone misses their train

5th movement 'Chaconne' from Partita in D minor for solo violin (BWV 1004) by Johann Sebastian Bach

... when a traveller comes home

1st movement 'Allegretto' from Symphony No. 2 in D major (Op. 43) by Jean Sibelius

... when someone stays awake all night thinking

2nd movement 'Andante' from Double Bass Concerto No. 2 in B minor by Giovanni Bottesini

... when there's a sad moment at a birthday party

2nd movement 'Adagio' from Sonata for Arpeggione and Piano in A minor (D. 821) by Franz Schubert

... when a baby is born

Aria 'Schafe können sicher weiden' ('Sheep May Safely Graze') *from Cantata (BWV 208) by Johann Sebastian Bach*

... at dusk

1st movement 'Fast' from New York Counterpoint by Steve Reich

... at dawn

1st Movement 'Erwachen heiterer Empfindungen bei der Ankunft auf dem Lande' ('Awakening of cheerful feelings on arrival in the countryside') *from Symphony No. 6 in F major (Op. 68) by Ludwig van Beethoven*

… at lunchtime when the ocean sparkles and glitters in the sun

1st movement from Piano Concerto by Germaine Tailleferre

… under a sky milky with stars

3rd movement 'Clair de lune' ('Moonlight') from Suite bergamasque (L. 75) by Claude Debussy

… when someone learns to ride a bike

Waltz in D-flat major 'Minute Waltz' No. 1 (Op. 64) by Frédéric Chopin

… when someone cooks dinner for six

'1B' by Edgar Meyer from the album 'Appalachian Journey' (Sony Music, 1999)

… when someone has lost their way in the middle of a cold and dark night

1st movement 'Poco Adagio' from Symphony No. 3 in C minor (Op. 78) by Camille Saint-Saëns

… just because someone is listening

Variation 9 'Nimrod' from Enigma Variations (Op. 36) by Edward Elgar

… when the music starts again, as beautiful as before

'The Lark Ascending' by Ralph Vaughan Williams

Alex Vaughan

Clare McFadden is a writer, artist and educator. She has worked in arts education with children, young people, and communities in both Australia and the United States. *The Flying Orchestra* was awarded the Children's Book Council of Australia Crichton Award, selected as one of the '50 Books You Can't Put Down', adapted for the stage as the headlining work at the Out of the Box Festival, and listed as one of the Australian Booksellers Association's '50 Favourite Kids' Books'. Clare holds a master's degree in education from Harvard University.

First published 2010 by University of Queensland Press
PO Box 6042, St Lucia, Queensland 4067 Australia
This paperback edition published 2019
Reprinted 2024

uqp.com.au
reception@uqp.com.au

Design and layout by Jo Hunt
Colour reproduction by Splitting Image
Printed in China by 1010 Printing International

ISBN (pbk) 978 0 7022 4929 7

NATIONAL LIBRARY OF AUSTRALIA
A catalogue record for this book is available from the National Library of Australia